R0083545665

09/2015

THE
KREE-SKRULL WAR

By Thomas Macri

Illustrated by Ramon Bachs *and* Hi-Fi Design

Based on the Marvel comic book series The Avengers

ABDO
Spotlight

MARVEL
New York

WWW.ABDOPUBLISHING.COM

Reinforced library bound edition published in 2015 by Spotlight, a division of ABDO
PO Box 398166, Minneapolis, Minnesota 55439. Spotlight produces high-quality
reinforced library bound editions for schools and libraries. Published by Marvel Press,
an imprint of Disney Book Group.

Printed in the United States of America, North Mankato, Minnesota.
052014
072014

marvelkids.com
© 2013 MARVEL

THIS BOOK CONTAINS
RECYCLED MATERIALS

LIBRARY OF CONGRESS CATALOGING-IN-PUBLICATION DATA

This title was previously cataloged with the following information:

Macri, Thomas.
The Avengers: the Kree-Skrull War / by Thomas Macri ; illustrated by Ramon Bachs and
Hi-Fi Design.
   p. cm. -- (World of reading. Level 3)
Summary: Conflict arises when the merciless Kree and the Skrulls go to war, placing the
Earth in danger as it waits for help from Captain Mar-Vell and the Avengers.
1. Avengers (Fictitious character)--Juvenile fiction. 2. Superheroes--Juvenile fiction. I.
Bachs, Ramon, ill. II. Hi-Fi Colour Design, ill. III. Title. IV. Series.
PZ7.M24731Kr 2013
[E]--dc23

2013935420

978-1-61479-265-9 (Reinforced Library Bound Edition)

Spotlight
A Division of ABDO
www.abdopublishing.com

Chapter One: Avengers No More!

Captain America, Thor, Iron Man, and the Hulk might be the most famous Avengers. But they aren't the only Avengers.

Once, the core Avengers were away.
Other members were on duty. A friend
of the team's was in trouble! They were
in New York City. He was in Miami.
They rushed to their Quinjet to find
him.

Among them was Vision. He was an android who could walk through walls. Quicksilver could run really fast.

Scarlet Witch had a hex power to make anything go her way. Hawkeye's eyes were as sharp as a hawk's. His arrows never missed their targets.

Their friend was Captain Mar-vell.

He was a Kree alien from another world. He had been stuck in a different dimension. He took on a lot of dangerous radiation there. The Avengers needed to help their friend. They arrived in Miami and found him. But Mar-vell didn't know he was in danger. He thought the Avengers were trying to attack him. So he fought them.

The Avengers knocked out their
friend to keep him from fighting them.

They brought him to a special lab.
They hooked him up to a machine. The
machine took away the radiation.

Soon, the public found out that there was an alien on Earth. They thought he was here to hurt them. A senator named Craddock wanted people to hunt down the aliens. But the team didn't turn over their friend, Mar-Vell.

Instead, they sent him away to hide.

People became angry at the Avengers. They thought they were traitors to Earth. The core group of Avengers arrived at the mansion. Captain America, Thor, Iron Man, and Hulk told Vision, Scarlet Witch, Quicksilver, and Hawkeye that they had disgraced the name of the Avengers. They said that they were breaking up the team— forever!

Chapter 2: The Avengers Return

The Avengers' Mansion was quiet and empty. And then a few days later Vision returned. He stormed into the mansion.

He was surprised to find Thor, Iron Man, Captain America, and Hulk inside. Why were they here? They had broken up the team! Before Vision could ask, he fell to the ground.

The Avengers didn't know what was wrong with him. They called Ant-Man and Wasp to help. They were Avengers, too.

Ant-Man and Wasp rushed to the mansion. They shrunk down. They were so small they could fit into the Vision's mouth. Then they went inside the android!

Being inside the Vision was like being in another world. The Super Heroes were attacked by strange things. These things seemed to have a mind of their own.

Finally, Ant-Man and Wasp made
their way to Vision's brain. They were
able to fix him. Ant-Man knew that he
and Wasp had to escape before Vision
woke up. If they didn't, Vision's body
would attack them!

They made it out of the Vision just
in time.

Vision woke up. The other Avengers asked where his teammates were.

Vision explained that they had been taken captive by a crew of aliens called Skrulls. Vision blamed the core Avengers for this. After all, they had broken up the team. They had sent him and his three teammates on their way.

But the other Avengers had no idea what he was talking about. This could only mean one thing. They knew the Skrulls could change the way they looked.

It must have been Skrulls pretending
to be the Avengers! They were the ones
who sent away the others. The team
checked their security recordings to
prove it. The Avengers needed to save
their teammates!

Chapter Three: Battleground Earth

But first they needed to find them. They needed any information they could get.

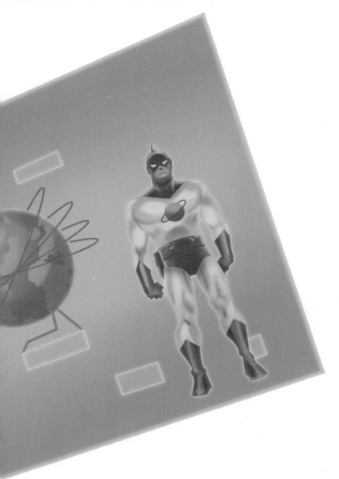

They learned that the Skrulls were at war with the Kree. They were the two strongest races in the universe. Earth was halfway between the Kree and Skrull worlds. This made it a very valuable prize. Whichever race controlled Earth would have a strategic place in the stars!

To make matters worse, the Kree's good leader, Supreme Intelligence, was being held captive. The evil Kree ruler, Ronan, had him locked up. Ronan ruled the Kree. Ronan loved war.

Meanwhile, on board a Skrull spacecraft, Scarlet Witch, Quicksilver, Hawkeye, and Mar-vell were held captive. The Skrulls thought that these heroes could be used to help them take Earth. They wanted to use Mar-vell. They wanted him to create a Kree weapon for them.

They tried to fool Mar-vell. They told him that the Skrulls would free his friends if he helped.

Back on Earth, Craddock was
still trying to get people to hate the
Avengers. He also wanted the people of
Earth to hate any alien. It didn't matter
if the alien was good or bad. People
were listening to him.

Things had never been worse for the
Avengers.

Chapter Four: War!

Then, things began to change. The core Avengers and Vision located the Skrull station where their friends were held. They rocketed off in their Quinjet.

Halfway there, the Avengers found
Ronan. He set an army of Kree warriors
against them. The Avengers fought
hard, and won.

Now the Supreme Intelligence could once again rule the Kree in peace. No longer would they wage war against the Skrulls.

But the Kree were only part of the problem. The Avengers continued their voyage. Then their ship came up against a huge fleet of Skrull vessels.

The Skrulls attacked
the Avengers.

The Avengers battled right back. They were only a few of Earth's mightiest heroes. They were fighting the most powerful army in the universe. Still, against all odds, the Avengers made it to the Skrull space station.

Meanwhile, Captain Mar-vell was working on his Kree weapon. Or, at least that's what the Skrulls thought. The Skrulls came to check on him. Mar-vell smashed the weapon. He freed his friends. And the battle began.

The team was together again at last.
The battle was long. The Avengers
fought hard.

Finally, they won! The Kree were now free from Ronan. The Skrulls were weakened. Peace had been restored.

The Avengers' work was done. They said good-bye to Mar-vell. They headed back to Earth.

Chapter Five: Home

The Avengers were welcomed home to cheers. The people of Earth loved them again. What had happened?

The Avengers learned that Craddock was actually a Skrull pretending to be a human! He was put on Earth to start trouble. When the people of the Earth discovered this, they locked him up. He was in a special jail. He couldn't ever escape.

The Earth was safe for the Avengers once more. And the Avengers had once again made the universe safe for the people of Earth!